KID SHERIFF AND THE TERRIBLE TOADS

written by **BOB SHEA**   illustrated by **LANE SMITH**

ROARING BROOK PRESS   NEW YORK, NEW YORK

For Ryan, the former sheriff of Bathytown
—B.S.

For Caroline and Zane Oakley
—L.S.

Text copyright © 2014 by Bob Shea
Illustrations copyright © 2014 by Lane Smith
Published by Roaring Brook Press
Roaring Brook Press is a division of Holtzbrinck Publishing Holdings Limited Partnership
175 Fifth Avenue, New York, New York 10010
mackids.com

Library of Congress Cataloging-in-Publication Data
Shea, Bob.
    Kid Sheriff and the terrible Toads / written by Bob Shea ; illustrated by Lane Smith. — First edition.
        pages cm
    Summary: The Toad brothers are wreaking havoc in Drywater Gulch when a boy with no experience
but immense knowledge of dinosaurs rides into town on his tortoise and declares himself the new sheriff.
    ISBN 978-1-59643-975-7 (hardback)
    [1. Robbers and outlaws—Fiction.   2. Sheriffs—Fiction.   3. Toads—Fiction.   4. Dinosaurs—
Fiction.   5 West (U.S.)—Fiction.   6. Humorous stories.]   I. Title.
PZ7.S53743Kid 2014
[E]—dc23
                                                                    2014001767

Roaring Brook Press books may be purchased for business or promotional use. For information on bulk
purchases please contact Macmillan Corporate and Premium Sales Department at (800) 221-7945 x 5442
or by email at specialmarkets@macmillan.com

First edition September 2014
Book design by Molly Leach
Printed in China by Toppan Leefung Ltd., Dongguan City, Guangdong Province

10   9   8   7   6   5   4   3   2   1

Drywater Gulch had
a toad problem.

Not the hop-down-your-britches kind of toad.

Not the croaking-all-night kind of toad.

The never-say-thank-you outlaw kind of toad.

Why, those Toad brothers would steal your gold, kiss your cattle, and insult your chili. Hootin', hollarin', and cussin' all the while.

Mayor McMuffin was beside his self. His cumin-scented town was a goner.

Then hope rode into town.

Slowly.
On a tortoise.

Give him a minute.

"Howdy stranger. What brings you to our spicy town?" asked the mayor.

"I'm your new sheriff," said the boy.

"Can you handle a shooting iron?"

"Nope."

"Ride a horse?"

"Nope."

"Know any rope tricks?"

"Nope."

"Stay up past eight?"

"Nope."

"Well then, what makes you a sheriff?" asked the mayor.

"I know a really lot about dinosaurs," said Ryan.

"Pleased to meet you, Sheriff," said the mayor.

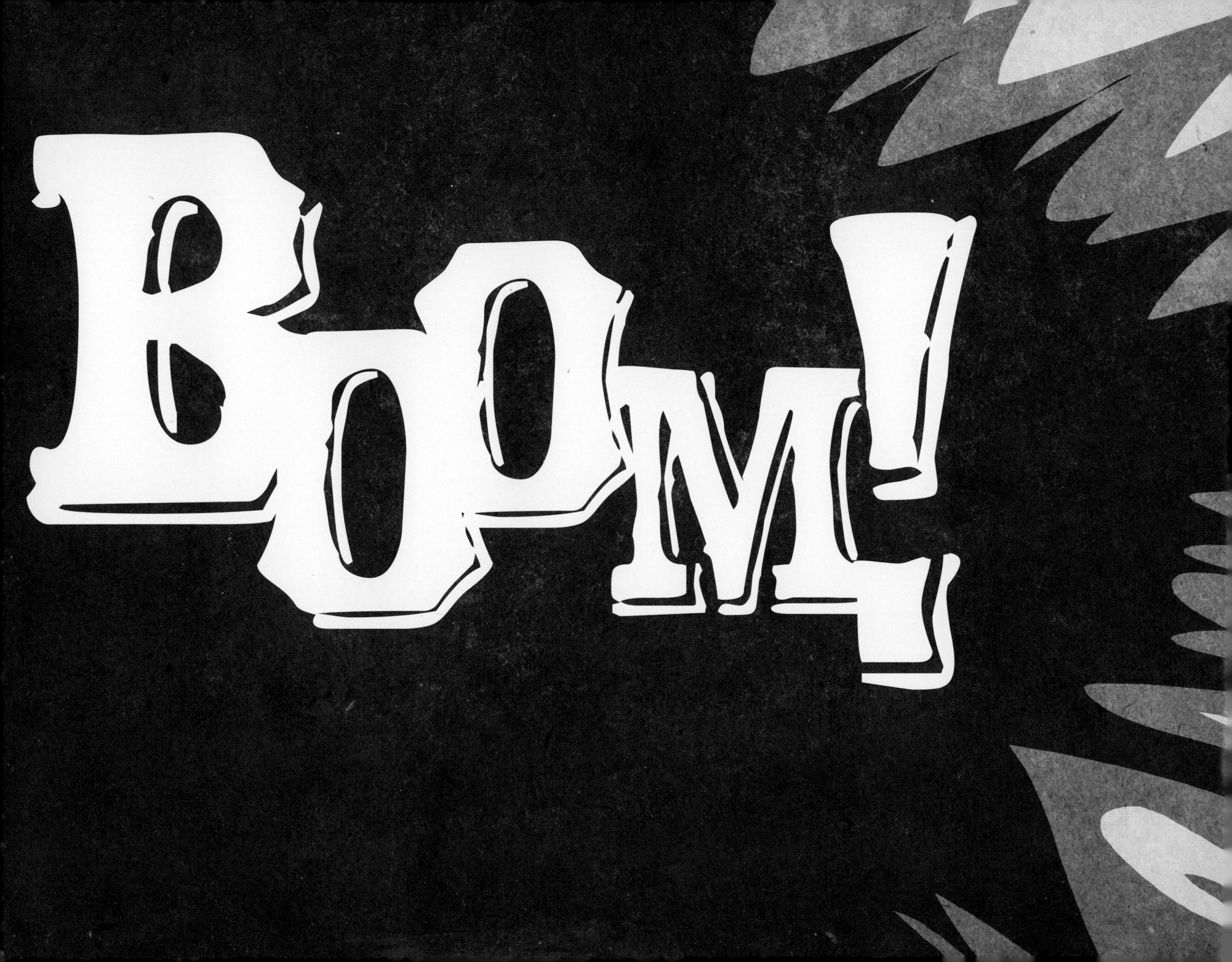
BOOM!

"The bank!" said the mayor. "The Toads!"

"A hole this big means one thing—T. rex,"
said the sheriff.

"Or dynamite," said the mayor.

"T. rex don't need no dynamite. Largest predator
of the Cretaceous period," said the sheriff.

"Wow, you're good," said the mayor.

"Quick! The stagecoach been robbed!"
a lady called.

"Whaddya reckon, Sheriff, T. rex?" asked the mayor.

"T. rex little baby arms ain't fit for the intricacies of knot tying," said Sheriff Ryan.

"So it were them Toads?" asked the mayor.

"Nope. Velociraptors. Whole mess a them. Confused your stagecoach with a lumbering Protoceratops, I reckon. Honest mistake."

"Why never once did I suspect dinosaurs while the Toads were a robbin' me. I feel mighty foolish," said Jimmy the stagecoach driver.

"Why I bet it were some crazy diney-o-saur what jumped my claim and stole my gold. Right, Sheriff?" said Gabby the town prospector.

"Nope," said the sheriff, "probably Toads. Don't be so quick to blame dinosaurs."

"That were wrong a me," said Gabby. "I'm powerful sorry."

"NOT AS SORRY AS Y'ALL GONNA BE!"

It were the Toads. Itchin' for some hootin', hollerin', and cattle kissin'.

"No time for your foolishness. Dinosaurs just robbed the bank," said the sheriff. "We got a cattle-kissin' Triceratops and a knot-tying, stagecoach-robbin' Velociraptor."

"What? That ain't right. We done robbed those!" said the big mean Toad.

"And weren't no try-lollipops kissin' them cattle neither. Why I smooched them beefy lips my own self!" said the big weird Toad.

"We been shoplifting from the mercantile all afternoon, too!" said the big ugly Toad.

"Allosaurus more likely," said the sheriff. "Sticky fingers."

"Oh yeah, then who's been insulting all the chili? Jerkosaurus rex?" said the big ugly Toad, who was also very, very funny.

"Stegosaurus," said the sheriff. "Herbivore. Only eats plants. Whip up a batch of vegetarian chili and he'd surely take a shine to it."

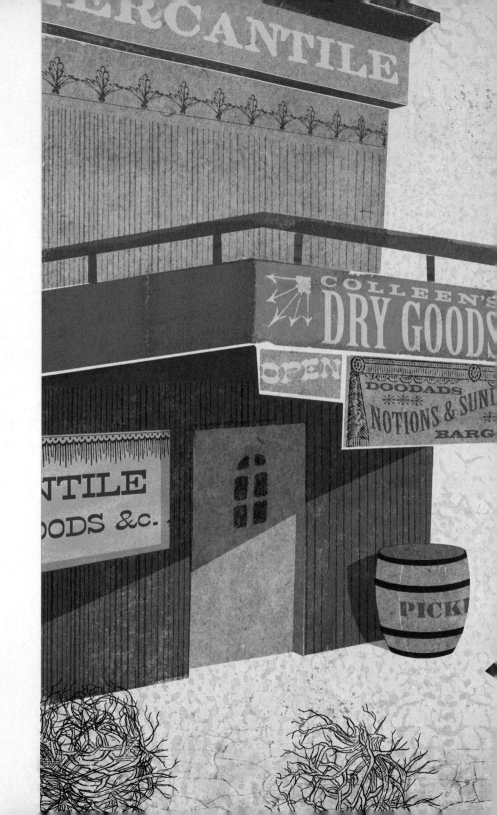

"That's enough!" said the big mean Toad. "We done all them crimes! Ain't fair giving the credit to no dineysaurs after the hard work we put in."

"Darn tootin'!" said the big weird Toad. "Cattle kissin' is downright disgustin'. I want what's comin' to me."

"Well, I reckon I could arrest you for being such a plumb nuisance, but I need this here jail for the real criminals. Dinosaurs are mighty big," said the sheriff.

"Real criminals? We'll show you!" said the big ugly Toad.

"OUTTA MY WAY!" said the big mean Toad.

"DINERSORES MY FOOT!" said the big weird Toad.

The Toads fought their way through the door of the jail, slamming it shut behind them.

"HA! You can blow them dinersores out your nose, Sheriff, this here jail is full up of real bonafide criminals!"

The sheriff locked the
jail good and tight.

"Hooray!"
the people cheered.

Sheriff Ryan saddled up his tortoise.

"Are you sure you can't stay? The town could use a good paleontologist," said the mayor.

"Sorry, Mayor," said Sheriff Ryan. "I'm a lawman."

Over the
next three days
he rode off into the sunset.